With special thanks to Natalie Doherty

For Al, who's always wanted me to write a book,
and for Sarah, for giving me the chance to do it.

Text copyright © 2015 by Hothouse Fiction
Illustrations copyright © 2015 by Sophy Williams

All rights reserved. Published by Scholastic Inc., 557 Broadway, New York, NY 10012, *Publishers since 1920.* SCHOLASTIC and associated logos are trademarks and/or registered trademarks of Scholastic Inc. Published by arrangement with Nosy Crow Ltd. Series created by Nosy Crow Ltd.

First published in the United Kingdom in 2013 by Nosy Crow Ltd., The Crow's Nest, 10a Lant St., SE1 1QR.

ISBN 978-0-545-84220-4

10 9 8 7 6 5 4 3 2   15 16 17 18 19/0

Printed in the U.S.A.   40
First edition, September 2015

Zoe's Rescue Zoo

The Lonely Lion Cub

Amelia Cobb

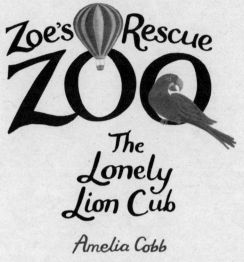

Illustrated by Sophy Williams

Scholastic Inc.

Chapter One
Zoe's Zoo

"Taroom! Taaarrrooomm! Tah-rah-rah-roomm!"

A deafening trumpeting noise blasted through the quiet early morning. It was so loud it made Zoe Parker's bedroom window rattle.

Zoe opened her eyes and grinned. "OK, OK, I'm up!" she said.

After a final stretch and wiggle of her
toes, she leaped out of bed. She pulled
on her jeans and a sparkly T-shirt before
putting on the necklace she always wore —
a pretty silver chain with a charm in
the shape of a lion's paw print. She
glanced in the mirror as she tugged
a brush through her
wavy brown hair
and smiled.

There were so many postcards tucked into the sides of the mirror frame that she could hardly see her reflection! Each card was from a faraway place and showed a different exotic animal. There were graceful gazelles in the African savanna, a shy baby panda from the Chinese mountains, and thousands of silver angelfish that sparkled like jewels in the Amazon river.

As another trumpet blast rang out, Zoe pulled on her shoes and glanced at her bed. "Where are you, sleepyhead?" she whispered. "Come out, come out, wherever you are . . ."

Everything was still for a moment. Then the covers at the bottom of the bed wiggled. "Aha," said Zoe as a small lump appeared and began to make its way up the bed. Then — ever so slowly — a pair of furry ears popped up from under the duvet. These were followed by a small, soft, pale-gray head with two huge, shiny golden eyes, blinking sleepily. Then, finally, a long, curly gray tail appeared.

"There you are, Meep." Zoe giggled as the tiny mouse lemur crept out from under the covers. "Wake up! It's breakfast time!"

"Meep! Meep!" the little lemur squeaked happily, suddenly wide awake. He scampered out of bed and jumped into Zoe's arms, chattering excitedly. She grinned as she held her fluffy friend.

There was another trumpeting sound,

and the little lemur jumped and grabbed on to Zoe's T-shirt. Zoe laughed again.

"Don't be silly, Meep, it's only Oscar," she said, flinging her window open.

Zoe grinned as she looked out over the patchwork of animal enclosures. From her bedroom she could see all the way from the shimmering lake where the hippos swam, over the grassy green fields full of striped zebras and tall, patterned giraffes, past the pond full of pink flamingos all standing on one leg, up to the windmill that powered the zoo with its sails turning in the wind, and all the way down to the elephant enclosure next door.

Zoe didn't think it was unusual to have a lemur sleeping at the end of her bed or an elephant in her backyard, because she lived in her great-uncle's zoo!

"Good morning to you too, Oscar," she called down happily.

The tip of a long, gray trunk appeared from behind a glossy banyan tree, followed by the tusks, head, and huge flapping ears of Oscar the African elephant. He lifted his trunk up high and waved at her, his wise old eyes twinkling. *"Taroom!"* he trumpeted again.

"No, Oscar, no school for me today. It's vacation," she called back. "Listen, I'll come and say hello later on, OK? And I'll bring you a treat if I can."

Elephants munched on tree bark, leaves, and grass most of the time, but Zoe knew they also loved sweet fruits like apples and oranges.

Oscar flapped his ears and gave a final happy trumpet.

"OK, I'll see if I can find you some bananas!" Zoe laughed.

Living at the Rescue Zoo wasn't the only amazing thing about Zoe's life. She also had a very special secret — she could talk to the animals!

Chapter Two
Zoe's Special Secret

Ever since Zoe's sixth birthday she'd been able to understand every squeak, roar, bellow, and bark that animals made.

She'd had a wonderful birthday party with her mom and her friends. The only thing that could have made it better would have been a visit from Great-Uncle Horace.

She had just been falling asleep that night when her mom called her name. Zoe ran down the stairs and burst into the lounge to see a familiar figure wearing khaki trousers, an explorer's hat, and a safari jacket with lots of pockets. His kind smile and twinkly eyes were framed by a bushy white beard. His parrot, Kiki, a large bird with bright-blue feathers, was perched on his shoulder.

"Great-Uncle Horace!" Zoe yelled, bounding up to him as he opened his arms and gave her a huge hug.

"Happy birthday, Zoe!" Horace smiled. "You didn't think I would miss it, did you?" His eyes twinkled as he handed her a package.

Excitedly, Zoe ripped open the paper to reveal a beautiful model of the Earth.

"Did you know that most of the world is covered in water?" Great-Uncle Horace asked her.

"Thank you for my present!" said Zoe, giving him a huge hug.

Great-Uncle Horace smiled. "Since you're so grown up now, I have a very important job for you. Can you look after Kiki while I talk to your mom about some zoo business?" He held out his arm and the parrot walked down it slowly, clutching his arm with her claws.

Great-Uncle Horace had rescued Kiki from South America when he was a young man and Kiki was just a tiny ball of fluffy feathers. They'd spent almost their whole lives together, and were as close as Zoe and Meep were. Great-Uncle Horace always said that Kiki was his good-luck

10

charm, and the beautiful macaw
went everywhere with him.
Great-Uncle Horace
tapped the top of
his suitcase, and
Kiki stepped off
his arm and
perched on
the handle.

"Hi, Kiki,"
Zoe said as
she stroked the
bird softly on
her head.

"Where have you
and Great-Uncle
Horace been this time?"

The macaw gave a squawk. But it
didn't *sound* like a squawk.

Zoe turned and looked at the bird curiously. "What did you say?" she asked.

Kiki squawked again, and Zoe gasped. She'd heard Kiki say, "Russia"!

Zoe shook her head in amazement — she could understand the bird as clearly as she could her mom and Great-Uncle Horace.

"But it was very cold," Kiki said as she shook her feathers with a shiver.

Zoe couldn't believe it. She'd *always* talked to the animals she met — but they'd never talked back before!

"Kiki!" she cried. "I can understand what you're saying!"

Kiki stared at Zoe, her dark eyes serious. Then she explained that animals spoke to people all the time, but only a few very special people understood them. She told Zoe that she couldn't tell *anyone* that animals could understand people, not even her mom or Great-Uncle Horace!

"You have to keep our secret," Kiki said with a loud squawk.

Zoe reached out and touched Kiki's soft tail feathers. It was amazing to be able to talk to animals! The old parrot nuzzled her hand, and Zoe looked into her wise eyes.

"OK, I promise," she said.

Ever since then, Zoe had kept her special gift a secret, making sure she only talked with the animals when she was alone with them. Soon after her amazing discovery, she and her mom had moved into the Rescue Zoo, and Zoe now had lots of animals to talk to and secretly help.

Meep nibbled her ear and Zoe stopped daydreaming with a jump.

"I'm hungry!" he squeaked.

"Meep!" Zoe scolded, gathering him gently into her arms and giving him a big good-morning hug. "I'm sure we can find you something tastier to eat than my ear!"

Giggling, Zoe skipped downstairs to the kitchen, with Meep holding on to her

14

shoulder and his long tail wrapped around her neck like a scarf.

First she made Meep's breakfast. While the little lemur sprang on to the table and bounced around, she chopped a banana into little pieces and added a sprinkle of sunflower seeds.

"Yum!" exclaimed Meep.

Then Zoe poured herself a bowl of cereal. As they ate, Zoe thought about the postcards around her mirror. They had all been sent by Great-Uncle Horace. He spent all his time traveling around the world searching for animals in need of help.

Whenever he found an injured or lost creature he'd bring it back to live at the Rescue Zoo. But it had been a long time since Great-Uncle Horace had come home with a new animal. Zoe knew he loved exploring and helping animals, but she always missed him when he was gone.

"I wonder where he is now." She sighed, resting her chin in the palm of her hand. "What do you think, Meep?"

Meep wrinkled his tiny nose as he thought carefully. "Maybe Goo is in Madagascar, where I came from?" he suggested, his mouth full. "Helping chameleons!"

Zoe smiled. She knew Meep only said "Goo" because he found "Great-Uncle Horace" a bit of a mouthful — but she thought it was very sweet! Zoe stroked him between his ears and Meep wriggled in delight.

"Maybe," she replied. "Or he could be rescuing flying foxes in Australia. Or . . . or—"

"I know! I know!" Meep jumped around excitedly, scattering bits of banana. "He's in the Specific, looking for tiger sharks!"

Zoe smiled. "You mean the *Pacific*. Great-Uncle Horace says that's the world's biggest, widest, deepest ocean."

She stopped eating when she heard the *crunch* of footsteps on the gravel path outside. Someone was coming. Zoe winked at Meep and put her finger to her lips.

Now they could hear a voice. A *furious* voice.

"Horrible, rude, little troublemakers! This is the *last straw*!"

Chapter Three
Mean Old Mr. Pinch

The door flew open and the zoo
manager, Percy Pinch, stormed into
the kitchen. Zoe gasped. Mr. Pinch was
normally very clean and tidy. His crisp
blue uniform was always neatly ironed,
his tie was perfectly straight, and his
black shoes so shiny that you could see
his pointy nose reflected in them.

But today he looked different. His uniform was splattered with smears and smudges. Pieces of kiwi fruit dripped from his shirt, mushed-up mango covered his pants, and there was banana on his cap. Mr. Pinch was *covered* in fruit!

"Hello, Mr. Pinch," said Zoe, trying not to laugh. "Have you been making a fruit salad?"

Meep exploded into giggles and Mr. Pinch glared at them both.

"This is an outrage!" he snapped. He was tall and skinny, with a thin mouth that always looked as if he had just accidentally eaten something bad.

Zoe's mom followed Mr. Pinch through the door. She was wearing her zoo uniform with RESCUE ZOO VET embroidered on the pocket under a symbol of a hot-air balloon. Her brown hair was pulled back into a ponytail, and she had a stethoscope around her neck. She took Mr. Pinch over to the sink, grabbed a damp cloth and helped him wipe the mess off his uniform.

"There, there, Mr. Pinch," she soothed. "We'll have you cleaned up in no time." She rolled her eyes at Zoe and smiled.

"Good morning, Zoe. Thanks for getting breakfast ready. And good morning to you too," she added as Meep chattered at her.

"My clean uniform is ruined!" Mr. Pinch moaned. "Those messy orangutans!"

Zoe couldn't understand why Mr. Pinch was so grumpy all the time. Being at the zoo made Zoe happier than anything else in the world, yet Mr. Pinch *never* smiled.

Last year Great-Uncle Horace had brought a tiny, fluffy, very rare white tiger named Sasha home from Siberia after he'd been injured in a trap. Sasha was one of the most beautiful creatures Zoe had *ever* seen, but Mr. Pinch had simply been annoyed. As all the other zoo staff rushed to meet the newcomer, he had muttered,

"*Ugh*, another cat! Doesn't Horace *know* I'm allergic?"

"Oh, the orangutans were just playing," Zoe's mom said.

Zoe grinned. *She* was sure the orangutans had thrown the fruit at Mr. Pinch on purpose!

"Exactly," Mr. Pinch said. "If we had less *playing*, things might stay clean. If you ask me, this zoo needs more rules and less fun."

"More rules, less fun! More rules, less fun!" Meep said cheekily, then blew a rude raspberry

22

that splattered Mr. Pinch with more banana bits.

Zoe burst out laughing. "Naughty Meep!" she whispered. "It's lucky he can't understand you!"

Mr. Pinch spluttered as he wiped globs of banana out of his eyebrows.

"That is exactly the type of behavior I'm talking about!" he blustered. "That creature should be in a cage!"

Meep shuddered and Zoe stroked his soft fur. She knew he was thinking about the tiny cage that he had been kept in until Great-Uncle Horace had found him and brought him to the Rescue Zoo. Even though Meep was now a happy little lemur, he still trembled every time he was inside a cage. He didn't even like the big enclosure that Great-Uncle

Horace had built for him, which was why he was allowed to spend all his time with Zoe.

Of course, Mr. Pinch wasn't very happy about that. He didn't even like *Zoe* being allowed to roam around the zoo, let alone Meep. Zoe usually tried to stay out of Mr. Pinch's way, but the zoo manager was always sneaking around, making sure that everyone was obeying the rules.

Zoe tickled Meep's belly as the little lemur shivered. There was no way she'd let Mr. Pinch take Meep away from her. Luckily her mom jumped in.

"Zoe, could you take this food package to the penguin enclosure? Little Poppy Penguin isn't feeling very well, so she needs to have a special diet." She glanced at her watch. "The zoo will open in a few minutes and I'd like Poppy to have her food before the visitors arrive."

"We have *real* zookeepers to do that kind of thing, you know," Mr. Pinch grumbled.

Zoe jumped up before he could say anything else. "OK, Mom," she said.

Meep leaped on to her shoulder and stuck out his tiny pink tongue at Mr. Pinch. Zoe grabbed the package and dashed outside. She sighed with relief as the door clicked shut, and set off into the Rescue Zoo. Zoe's cottage was right at the entrance to the zoo, just inside the big gates that were decorated with all kinds of animal carvings.

The gates would soon be open, letting in a stream of visitors. The first thing visitors always saw was a beautiful signpost standing next to Zoe's cottage. It was

wooden and had golden
arrows pointing the
way to different
parts of the zoo.
On top of the
signpost was a
golden hot-air
balloon — the symbol
of the Rescue Zoo.

Beyond the signpost,
a redbrick path led straight
ahead and then wound
around the zoo. Wooden
walkways
connected the
path to each
animal
enclosure.

A tall oak fence surrounded the zoo. It was topped with solar panels, which glittered in the sunlight. Great-Uncle Horace liked the Rescue Zoo to be kind to the environment as well as to the animals who lived there.

"Come on, Meep," Zoe said, smiling as she set off down the path. "We've got some special food for a sick penguin."

And from the sound of the roars, growls, yaps, and squawks floating toward her, it seemed like Poppy wasn't the only animal in the Rescue Zoo who was ready for breakfast!

Chapter Four
The Penguin Puzzle

Zoe and Meep headed toward the penguin enclosure. Walking through the zoo was like visiting all the different countries of the world. They passed a warm stretch of golden sand dotted with prickly cacti where the zoo's herd of camels lived. After that was a steamy green forest of lush trees and rare wildflowers, full of

chattering capuchin monkeys.
Great-Uncle Horace wanted each
animal's enclosure to be as much like
their home in the wild as possible.

Zoe couldn't resist stopping at one
particular enclosure. It was shaped like
a huge white igloo. As Zoe went inside,
she shivered in the cool air and rubbed
her arms, which were suddenly covered
in goose bumps. Meep's teeth chattered
noisily.

Inside the igloo was a platform where
visitors could look down on a large,
sapphire-blue pool. Twinkling icicles hung
from the ceiling. Toward the back, a snow
machine made a soft humming sound as
it blew out a gentle patter of white flakes.
Apart from that, everything was quiet.

Zoe glanced around to make sure

nobody was nearby. She leaned
on the railing.

"Hello?" she called. "Bella, are
you there?" As she spoke, her breath
misted in the freezing-cold air.

A ripple appeared on the pond's
surface and a small white head
appeared with a splash.

"Grrr, grr!" Bella growled
playfully as she paddled toward
Zoe.

Bella was one of Zoe's favorite
animals. She was a sassy little polar
bear cub with the whitest, fluffiest fur
Zoe had ever seen. She looked up at Zoe
with her bright brown eyes and growled
again.

"Of course I want to see you dive!"
Zoe told her. "Have you been practicing?"

With a grunt, the polar bear flipped upside down and disappeared into the deep water. She twirled happily and then shot back up to the surface.

"Amazing, Bella!" Zoe laughed as the bear splashed around the pool. "We have to take something to one of the penguins now," Zoe said, "but we'll see you later, OK?"

Bella wriggled her ears and gave a good-bye grunt as she plunged back under the water.

As they left the igloo, Zoe started to walk faster. She was about to reach the only enclosure that she didn't like walking by. It was a warm golden plain, fringed with the long, green grass of the Kenyan savanna.

This was the home of Leonard, the East

African lion. He was a large, powerful animal with a beautiful mane. But he also had curved teeth that he liked to show off and he could be very grumpy. Zoe's mom said it was because he had been treated very badly by people. He had been captured by dangerous poachers back in Kenya and taken to a city called Nairobi, where he wasn't given enough to eat or drink. Leonard was very lucky to be alive when Great-Uncle Horace rescued him.

Zoe wasn't scared of any animal but Leonard always made her a little nervous. She had never even talked to him because every time she went near his enclosure he roared so loud that even people that couldn't understand animals knew it meant, "GO AWAY!"

Zoe saw Leonard lying down on a grassy mound, resting his head on his giant paws. Spotting Zoe and Meep, he growled at them before yawning widely. Meep squeaked at the sight of his big sharp teeth and huddled against Zoe.

Zoe hurried past. She could feel Meep shaking and she gave him a quick hug.

"It's all right," she whispered. "He can't hurt you."

"He is a *little* scary," Meep admitted, jumping out of Zoe's arms and scampering along the path in front of her. "But I bet that grumpy old lion couldn't catch me anyway!" He raced away and Zoe followed him, laughing.

The chatter and noise around the zoo were steadily growing. The gates were now open and the first visitors of the day were starting to arrive. One little girl with blonde braids stared in amazement at Meep and Zoe walking along together, and tugged at her big sister's hand.

"Look!" she whispered. "A tiny monkey!"

Zoe smiled at her. "Meep's a gray

mouse lemur," she explained. "Meep, come and say hello."

Meep scampered up to Zoe and jumped on to her shoulder.

The little girl shyly reached out her hand to stroke Meep's tail, then jumped back and hid behind her sister with a giggle.

"He's so soft!" Zoe heard the little girl yell as they waved good-bye and continued along the path.

Zoe stopped when they reached the penguin enclosure. One of the walls was made out of glass so that visitors could see the penguins swimming and diving underwater. But today the whole colony was perched on the rocks, squawking. They were all talking at the same time so Zoe couldn't understand them.

"What are they saying?" she asked Meep. "It sounds like 'loon'."

Meep shrugged and gave a chattering laugh. "Loon! Loon!" he chirped, copying the penguins.

"Peggy! Pearl!" Zoe called softly to the nearest penguins. "Are you OK? I can't understand you! What does 'loon' mean?"

But the penguins couldn't hear her above the noise. Then Zoe spotted Will, the penguin-keeper, standing in the enclosure with a bucket of fish.

"Hi, Will!" she called. "Here's some special food for Poppy."

"Thanks, Zoe," Will replied. "I'm going to have trouble getting her to eat though. She's acting as strangely as the rest of them. They all seem really excited about something."

Zoe glanced at the penguins and
wondered if she could distract Will
somehow so that she could talk to them.
But before she could think of a plan,
there was another burst of noise. The
penguins were all hopping up and down,
flapping their flippers and staring up at
the sky, squawking wildly.

Will, Zoe, and Meep
looked up. Suddenly
Zoe understood what
the penguins had been
saying. Not "loon," but
"*balloon*!" A huge rainbow-colored
hot-air balloon soared overhead.
Underneath the balloon was a large
wicker basket, and attached to *that*
was a wooden crate. Meep squeaked in
excitement and scrabbled up on to Zoe's
head, reaching his hands into the air.

As the balloon floated over their heads,
Zoe turned and ran back through the
zoo, grinning.

Only one person she knew traveled by
hot-air balloon — Great-Uncle Horace!

Chapter Five
A New Arrival

With Meep scampering in front of her,
Zoe raced toward the wide clearing in
front of the gift shop where the balloon
always landed.

"Goo's back! Goo's back!" the lemur
chirped, his tail waving in excitement.

Zoe knew that Meep had missed
Great-Uncle Horace just as much as she

had, and he wasn't the only one. As she ran past each enclosure she heard brays and whinnies and squeaks of excitement. All the animals had spotted the balloon, and they knew what it meant! Great-Uncle Horace had helped every single creature in the Rescue Zoo, and they all loved it when he came home. Every animal was celebrating!

Zoe was already thinking about the crate beneath the hot-air balloon. What animal could be inside? Zoe and Meep reached the clearing just as the balloon landed.

A crowd of visitors had gathered in the clearing, and the air was filled with a buzz of curious chatter. All the zoo staff had rushed to greet Great-Uncle Horace as well, and to see what the new arrival might be. Even Mr. Pinch was there, eyeing the wooden crate suspiciously.

Zoe's mom ran over to join Zoe. She hugged her daughter happily. "Thank goodness he's back safely!" She smiled.

There was a movement from the wicker basket as someone threw out a thick rope ladder.

Zoe beamed as her great-uncle appeared. His old green hat was still perched wonkily on his head, and he was wearing the same sandy-colored safari jacket with lots of pockets for storing things, such as a map, a pair of binoculars, and a box of his favorite cookies. He was the smartest person Zoe had ever met, and she was sure he knew more about animals than anyone else in the world.

He waved at the crowd as he climbed down the rope ladder, and smiled when he spotted Zoe.

"Hello, everyone!" he said. "*Jambo!* That's Swahili for 'hello,' you know. Sorry I've been away for such a long time. I've been to Norway. Did you know that reindeer are called 'caribou' in Norway? It must be very confusing for Rudolph. And then I got an urgent call from Kenya about a new animal for the Rescue Zoo!"

The moment he reached the bottom of the ladder, Zoe ran to her great-uncle and threw herself at him. Great-Uncle Horace swept her up and whirled her around.

"Zoe, my dear!" he cried, hugging her warmly. "It's wonderful to see you. Look how much you've grown! And here's

44

your little partner-in-crime," he added, as Meep leaped on to his shoulder and snuggled up to his beard. "Hello, Meep. I hope you've been behaving yourself."

There was a squawk and a flurry of blue feathers as a beautiful parrot sailed down and landed on Great-Uncle Horace's shoulder. She pecked at Meep, who jumped into Zoe's arms, chattering grumpily.

"Now, now, Kiki," Great-Uncle Horace said, tapping the bird gently on her curved black beak. "Meep was only saying hello to me."

Kiki glared suspiciously at Meep. Zoe laughed as the lemur stuck his tongue out at the elderly bird. Although they both loved their owners, Kiki and Meep didn't like each other very much!

"Now, where's our talented vet?"
Horace continued once Kiki was settled
on his shoulder.

Zoe's mom ran over to hug her uncle.
"Welcome home," she said.

"We've got *so* much to tell you, Great–
Uncle Horace," Zoe began. "The new
panda enclosure was finished last month,
and Su Lin loves it! The baby llamas are
doing really well, and Bella the polar
bear is getting so big." Her words tumbled
out in a rush, and Great–Uncle Horace
laughed. Zoe felt as if she could have
talked for days, filling him in on all the
news from the zoo.

"You really shouldn't stay away so long,"
Zoe's mom scolded her uncle. "We didn't
know if you were ever coming home."

Great–Uncle Horace shook his head.

46

"My dear, you worry far too much. I've just been busy. I met so many animals who needed my help, you see — especially when I arrived in Kenya. A truly amazing place." He nodded at Zoe. "When you're a little bit older, you must come with me. I think you'd love it."

Zoe grinned excitedly. She couldn't wait to join her great-uncle on his amazing adventures!

"Ahem." Mr. Pinch stepped forward, clearing his throat as if he was about to make an important speech. "Mr. Higgins. Now that you're back, sir, there are some very urgent zoo matters to attend to. First of all, I would like to talk to you about the habits of some of the animals. The orangutans, for example —"

Zoe looked from Great-Uncle Horace to the crate and back again. She just wanted to meet the new arrival! She hopped from one foot to the other impatiently. Great-Uncle Horace noticed her eagerness and smiled.

"Ah, Mr. Pinch," he interrupted. "I'm sure you're doing a splendid job of looking after the zoo without me sticking my old nose in." He peered around through his binoculars. "Yes,

yes. Everything looks to be under control."

Mr. Pinch turned very pink and beamed smugly. He puffed out his chest importantly and looked around at the staff to make sure they had all heard. Meep squealed with laughter, almost falling off Zoe's shoulder.

"Silly old Pinch," he said. "He looks like one of the owls when they fluff up their feathers to stay warm!"

Zoe spluttered with laughter. Meep was right!

"Now, you must all be desperate to meet the new arrival," Great-Uncle Horace announced, patting the wooden crate. "I found this poor little fellow all alone in the Serengeti. The rest of his family had been captured by poachers."

He shook his head sadly. "Without anyone to look after him, he would almost certainly have died. I just *had* to rescue him."

Great-Uncle Horace nodded to the zookeepers standing in the crowd. Three of them cut away the thick ropes fastening the crate. Meep jumped up on Zoe's head to try and get a better view. What could the new animal be?

Great-Uncle Horace lifted up one of the sides of the crate and the crowd gasped. Zoe's heart leaped. Behind her, she heard Mr. Pinch groan.

A furry little animal with rounded ears, chocolate-brown eyes, and a long tail with a brown tuft on the end peered out from inside the crate. It was a fluffy lion cub!

Chapter Six
Zoe's Promise

The cub blinked nervously at the crowd. He opened his mouth to reveal a row of white baby teeth and gave a squeaky growl. His little paws trembled and he looked very weak and frightened.

"Stand back, please!" Mr. Pinch announced as the visitors pushed forward to get a better look. "Make way for the vet."

Zoe's mom knelt down slowly next to the cub. "There, there, little one. I'm not going to hurt you," she soothed as she examined the lion's eyes, ears, teeth, tummy, and paws. The cub shrank away, snarling as fiercely as he could. Zoe's mom looked up. "You found him just in time, Uncle Horace. It looks like he hasn't eaten in weeks."

Zoe and Meep shared a worried look. The cub seemed confused and very scared. He kept turning his head from side to side, as if he was looking for someone in the crowd. Zoe desperately wanted to explain that everyone at the Rescue Zoo was really kind and wanted to help him. But she couldn't talk to him in front of the crowd — she had to keep the animals' secret.

Zoe felt a gentle tug on her hair, and realized it was Kiki trying to get her attention.

Great-Uncle Horace was standing next to her. Leaning closer, he whispered, "My dear, this little chap needs help. Will you promise to look after him for me?"

Zoe stared at her great-uncle and then

nodded. "I promise. I'll try my very best to help the cub."

Great-Uncle Horace beamed at her. "That's my girl, Zoe! I know you can do it." He smiled brightly as Kiki nibbled his ear.

"OK!" he announced. "Let's see what's been going on around here while I've been gone. I must say hello to all the animals right away. First, a trip to visit Charles, I think. I do miss that old fellow when I'm on my travels. Did you know, everyone, that giant tortoises like Charles can live to be over two hundred years old? Incredible!" Great-Uncle Horace waved to the crowd, winked at Zoe, then strode off happily down the path toward the tortoise enclosure.

Kiki spread her wings
and soared across to
Zoe from Great-Uncle
Horace's shoulder and
circled over her head.
Something light and
soft floated down into
Zoe's hand. It was one
of Kiki's bright,
beautiful blue tail feathers.

Zoe tucked it safely into her
pocket. Kiki was Great-Uncle
Horace's lucky charm, and it was almost
as if the macaw was saying, "Good luck!"
to her. Great-Uncle Horace had asked
her to help the little lion cub — and she
was determined to keep her promise.

Once Great-Uncle Horace was out
of sight, Zoe's mom clapped her hands

together. "Let's get the cub to the zoo hospital," she called. "He needs food and water right away."

A zookeeper brought over a special blanket, which Zoe's mom gently wrapped around the frightened lion cub. She scooped him up and headed straight for the hospital, weaving her way through the chattering crowd.

Zoe knew the blanket would keep the animal toasty warm and would also protect her mom's hands from any scratches. She followed, with Meep scampering along beside her.

"Ahem!"

A bony finger tapped her on the shoulder. Zoe's heart sank as she turned to see Mr. Pinch glaring at her. Zoe noticed he still had a smudge of banana on his forehead.

"And just where do you think *you're* going?" he sneered.

"I was going to the hospital —" Zoe began.

Mr. Pinch narrowed his eyes. "Young lady, the hospital is for *zoo staff only*. Whenever Horace brings back a new arrival it creates lots of paperwork, and it's up to me to keep the zoo running smoothly. So I will *not* have an unruly little girl and a troublemaking lemur getting in the way!" he said, pointing at Meep.

Meep squeaked and made a very rude noise, as if to prove just how troublesome he could be.

Zoe nodded sadly. No matter how helpful she tried to be, Mr. Pinch always told her she was causing trouble. But as soon as Mr. Pinch was out of sight, an idea popped into her head.

"Don't worry, Meep," she whispered. "With Pinch busy at the hospital, we can tell the other animals all about the new arrival."

Suddenly she felt much better!

Chapter Seven
Welcome to the Rescue Zoo!

Zoe and Meep headed right for the nearest animal enclosure — a warm, golden field dotted with wild apricot trees where the giraffe family lived.

A little boy with curly black hair was standing on the wooden walkway leading to the fence, taking a picture. As Zoe stepped on to the walkway, the youngest giraffe spotted her and trotted right up to the fence. The little boy gasped to see the beautiful animals so close, and Zoe smiled at him.

"Did you know that all giraffes have a different pattern of special markings along their long necks and bodies, so once you get to know them all, you can tell them apart?" she said. "This one is Daisy."

"Cool!" the boy said.

Zoe waited until the boy and his parents had moved on to the next enclosure so she could speak to Daisy without them noticing. She pulled her paw-print necklace out from under her T-shirt and held it against a small panel in the wall of the giraffe house. There was a click and the door swung open.

The necklace wasn't just a pretty piece

of jewelery — the paw-print charm had a special electronic chip inside it which opened the gate to every enclosure in the Rescue Zoo. All the staff had paw-print-shaped passes that let them into the private areas of the zoo, and Great-Uncle Horace had had one made into a necklace especially for Zoe.

As Zoe stepped into the giraffe house, Daisy galloped in through the huge door and ran around in a circle, swishing the tassel on the end of her tail.

"So you've already heard the news?" Zoe chuckled, stroking Daisy's velvety nose.

The giraffe gazed at Zoe with huge, shiny black eyes and blinked her beautiful long lashes.

"Yes, it's a tiny lion cub!" Zoe said.

"But he seems really unhappy. I wonder what we can do to help."

Daisy nibbled Zoe's fingers very gently.

Zoe laughed. "You're right! Giving him some treats might help him settle in. He might like a bottle of warm milk to drink — we had to make sure Bella the polar bear had lots of milk when she was very small. I wonder if a blanket would help too."

"*Mmm*, blanky," Meep agreed, burying his face in Zoe's hair. "That will make the cub feel better!"

Zoe giggled. "I know that's what would make *you* happy, little Meep! Come on — let's collect everything we think will help him feel at home!"

When Zoe's mom arrived back at the cottage that evening, Zoe and Meep were waiting eagerly in the kitchen.

"Mom!" Zoe called. "We're in here. We've collected some things for the lion cub to help him settle in."

They carefully arranged the items on the kitchen table. There was a piece of tire, a ball, and a rope for him to play with, and a thick, cuddly blanket.

Once Zoe's mom had inspected everything, she kissed her daughter on her forehead. "I'm *very* impressed," she said. "You'll make a fantastic vet one

day, Zoe — you
certainly care
about the
animals
enough!
But I'm
afraid the
cub needs
much more
than a cozy
blanket. He won't eat *anything*, and it
means he's really weak. If things don't
change soon, he could become very sick."
Zoe's mom shook her head sadly. "We
just can't figure out what the problem is."

As Zoe's mom took greens from the
fridge to make dinner, Zoe glanced at
Meep. If anyone at the Rescue Zoo could
find out what was troubling the little cub,

she could — but it wouldn't be that easy. Mr. Pinch had forbidden her from visiting the cub, and she knew he would be sneaking around the hospital all day long. How could she get inside without him knowing?

In a flash of inspiration, Zoe knew exactly what she had to do. She'd never get past Mr. Pinch in the daytime — so she would just have to go to the hospital at night! She'd be in big trouble if Mom and Mr. Pinch found out, but she couldn't think of any other way to see the cub alone.

Zoe turned to Meep, her eyes shining. "I've got it!" she whispered. "We're going to the hospital tonight — as soon as Mom's asleep!"

Chapter Eight
Zoe's Nighttime Adventure

As soon as Zoe heard her mom snoring, she and Meep crept downstairs and out of the front door. Night had fallen over the Rescue Zoo, so Zoe turned on her flashlight. The air was still warm, and she could hear soft noises floating across the zoo. The last visitors had gone home hours ago, but lots of the animals were nocturnal, which meant that they slept during the day and were wide awake at night. The Rescue Zoo never really went to sleep!

As they walked toward the hospital, Zoe's heart thumped excitedly. She wanted to skip and run around, but she made herself walk quietly. If her mom found out that she'd sneaked away, she'd be furious. Even worse, Zoe knew that Mr. Pinch sometimes patrolled the zoo when it was dark, making sure none of his rules were being broken.

If Mr. Pinch spotted them tonight, Zoe knew he would finally do what he'd always threatened: He'd put poor Meep in a cage and forbid Zoe from walking around the zoo without a grown-up. Just thinking about it gave her a horrible

feeling in her stomach. But she had
promised Great-Uncle Horace that she'd
help the lion cub, and this was the only
way she could talk to him alone.

Zoe crept closer to the hospital. She
loved the Rescue Zoo, but it felt different
at night and a teeny bit scary. She was
so used to the path bustling with visitors
that it was strange to be the only person
around. She jumped as she heard a
squeak from the enclosure next to her.

"Silly Zoe, it's only the bumblebee bats,"
Meep said, jumping out of her arms. Zoe
calmed down as she watched the bats
swooping around in the moonlight,
enjoying the warm air.

Zoe shushed them as they
called out to her in their
high-pitched squeaks.

"I know we're out late. We're on a secret mission!"

The bats squeaked and squealed again, quietly this time, as they wished Zoe and Meep luck.

Meep leaped along in front of her, jumping in and out of the beam of light her flashlight made on the path in front of them. The little lemur wasn't afraid at all — his sharp eyes could see just as well in the dark as they could in the daytime.

The zoo hospital was a cozy bungalow painted a cheerful yellow, but in the darkness it looked cold and gray. Zoe switched off the flashlight and pressed her paw-print necklace to the sensor. The door opened with a click and she slipped inside with Meep, breathing a sigh of relief.

Zoe tiptoed beside a row of large pens filled with sleeping animals, smiling as she passed a meerkat with a bandaged paw, a snoring zebra, and some young monkeys all sleeping in a heap.

Zoe's mom always put the sickest patients right at the end of the hallway, where it was quiet — and that was where Zoe found the lion cub.

He was curled in a fluffy ball on a heap of blankets. Next to him was a bowl full of meat, and it didn't look as if he'd eaten any of it. His face was hidden beneath his paws and he was mewing quietly. Zoe realized that he was crying so she hurried to the pen and knelt down next to him.

"Don't cry!" she whispered. "We've come to help you."

The cub raised his head and stared at Zoe with big, dark eyes. His ears pricked up curiously.

73

Meep moved closer to the cub. "I'm Meep, and this is my best friend, Zoe," he said. "She can understand us. What's your name?"

The cub hesitated and then growled softly in reply.

"Rory," repeated Zoe, smiling. "That's a nice name. There's no need to be frightened, Rory. This is a very special place, and we all want to make sure you're happy and safe. Can you tell us what's wrong?"

The lion gulped nervously. Zoe waited, hoping that he would trust her.

Slowly, Rory began to explain. He had lived with his mom and his sister in the Serengeti with the rest of their pride. One day, Rory woke up early feeling thirsty, so he left his family's den to have a drink

of water from the nearby lake. While he
was gone, he heard roars and lots of men
shouting, followed by some scary bangs.
He waited until the noises had stopped,
then crept back to the den. His pride
had gone and he was left all alone.
Meep shuddered as Rory came to the
end of his story.

"That's awful," Zoe said, gazing at
the cub. "I know you must miss your
family *so* much," she whispered. "I promise
everything will be all right, now that
you're here. But please can you eat
something? My mom says you'll get
really sick if you don't."

Rory shook his head and hid his
eyes under his paws again.

Zoe tried her best to coax him out.

"Please, Rory, just try a few bites."

She nodded at the bowl next to him. "It will help you get better."

"If you don't like it, there's lots more yummy food at the Rescue Zoo," Meep added helpfully. "You can have anything you want!"

But Rory's face stayed firmly hidden. Meep looked at Zoe sadly.

"It's not working," he whispered. "What should we do?"

"I think we should let Rory get some rest," Zoe replied. "We'll try to come back tomorrow, Rory," she added, and heard a tiny snore from inside the pen. The tired cub had already fallen asleep.

Zoe sighed as they crept back to the cottage. "This is really serious, Meep. He misses his family so much. I think he's just too lonely to eat."

"But what can we do?" asked Meep, wrinkling his nose. "We can't bring his family back."

"No," agreed Zoe thoughtfully. "We can't. But there has to be *something* we can do."

Chapter Nine
A Lonely Lion

Zoe didn't sleep very well that night.
As Meep snoozed peacefully at the end
of her bed, wrapped around her feet like
a furry hot-water bottle, she lay awake
worrying about Rory. There *had* to be
a way to help him.

Zoe's mom had already left when they
came downstairs for breakfast the next

morning. There was a note on the kitchen table.

GONE TO CHECK ON THE CUB. COME TO THE HOSPITAL TO SAY HELLO IF YOU WANT — MR. PINCH WILL BE AT THE HIPPO ENCLOSURE ALL MORNING CLEANING UP AFTER HETTY!

MOM xxx

Zoe smiled. Hetty was the smallest and naughtiest of the hippopotamuses, and one of her favorite things to do was splash gloopy mud around her enclosure. It made Mr. Pinch very angry!

Zoe and Meep quickly munched their breakfast and set off into the zoo. As usual, the animals called out to her cheerfully, but Zoe barely heard them — she just couldn't stop thinking about Rory. Meep did his best to make her laugh by doing cartwheels along the path, but Zoe only managed a sad smile.

As they drew closer to Leonard's enclosure, Meep's teeth began to chatter. "I wish we didn't have to go past the grumpy old lion," he muttered.

Zoe bent down and tickled his ears. "Remember he can't hurt you, Meep," she reminded him.

"I know," grumbled Meep. "But why does he always roar like that? No wonder he has that big enclosure all to himself. Nobody wants to be his friend!"

Zoe stopped. Her heart was beating very fast. "Meep — that's it!" she cried. "*That's* how we can help Rory!"

"What? How?" asked Meep, puzzled.

"Rory is lonely — that's why he's so sad.

He misses his family and being around other lions," Zoe explained. "But we have another lion at the zoo already — Leonard! He comes from Kenya, just like Rory. If we can get Leonard to share his enclosure with Rory, everything would be perfect."

"But Leonard is the grumpiest, growliest animal in the whole zoo," Meep said. "He won't listen to you, Zoe. He'll just roar at you!"

Zoe nodded. "I know. But I have to try."

Poor Meep looked terrified, so Zoe picked him up and nuzzled his soft head reassuringly. "Maybe we should find you a good place to sit farther back down the path?" she suggested. She knew Meep wouldn't want to come too close to Leonard's enclosure.

Zoe set Meep down on a wooden bench where he would still be able to see her. He curled up and covered his face, peeking out nervously from behind his tail.

Zoe went back to the edge of the walkway that led to Leonard's enclosure. She looked around to check there were no visitors coming along the path. Taking a deep breath, she closed her eyes for a moment. *You can do this*, she told herself firmly. She reached into her pocket and found the blue feather Kiki had given her. Maybe it would bring her luck. Clutching it tightly, she stepped bravely onto the walkway and went toward the fence.

The huge old lion was prowling around his enclosure.

Zoe cleared her throat. "Um . . . excuse

me," she said in a timid whisper. "Can I please talk to you?"

Leonard spun around to face Zoe. His golden eyes glared at her and he let out a small, low growl from deep in his throat. He pressed his ears flat against his head, warning her not to come any closer. Zoe stayed very still.

"A new animal came to the Rescue Zoo yesterday," she said. "His name is Rory. He's a lion, like you, but he's just a baby. He lived with his family in a big pride, but now he's all alone."

When Zoe said the word "pride" Leonard's ears pricked up. He was still staring at her, but he wasn't growling any more.

"He won't eat anything because he's so sad, and it's making him sick," Zoe continued shakily. "He needs a new home, and someone to share it with."

Leonard gazed at Zoe for a moment. He tipped his handsome head to one side, as if remembering something. Then he growled, making a deep, purring rumble.

Zoe couldn't believe the lion was really talking to her! She listened carefully, and as she watched Leonard's eyes gleam, she saw that he looked . . . happy.

Meep crept closer as he realized that Leonard was talking to Zoe. "What's he saying?" Meep chirped nervously, peeking at the lion from behind Zoe's legs.

"Leonard used to belong to a big pride, just like Rory," Zoe explained. "There were two lions and ten lionesses, and they helped to keep one another safe." She glanced at the lion. "He was so happy . . . until the poachers came and took him away. Meep, I think *Leonard* is lonely too."

Without warning, Leonard bared his teeth and let out an enormous roar that sent Meep scurrying back down the path.

It was as if the lion had decided he didn't want to think about his pride any more. With an angry swish of his tail, he turned and stormed away from the fence.

"Wait!" Zoe pleaded. "Leonard, come back! I think we can help. You miss your pride and living with other lions. Rory's all alone too, and he needs a home. Couldn't you share your enclosure with him?"

But the lion wasn't listening any more.

Zoe sighed and walked back on to the path. Meep jumped straight up into her arms for a cuddle. "Poor Leonard," Zoe said. "He looked so happy when he was remembering his old pride. He must miss them so much."

"Maybe he's not as mean as we

thought," Meep admitted. "But he's still grumpy and scary when he roars!"

"He is," Zoe agreed. "But now we know why he behaves like that. He's sad and lonely, and he needs a friend . . . just like Rory." She nibbled her lip thoughtfully. "I'm *sure* my plan will work, Meep."

Meep looked worried. "But we don't know if Leonard *wants* to share his home with another lion!"

Zoe sighed. "I wish we knew for sure. But I don't think Leonard will talk to me again." She glanced back at him and took a determined breath. "But we have to try, somehow. Come on, Meep — let's go to the zoo hospital. We need to talk to my mom — and to Rory!"

Chapter Ten
Zoe's Plan

When Zoe and Meep arrived at the
hospital, Zoe's mom was busy wrapping
a bandage around a koala's paw.

"Hello, Mom! Can we go and see
the lion cub?" asked Zoe.

Zoe's mom hesitated. "Well . . . I guess
it won't do any harm. Be nice and quiet

around him, OK? We don't want him to get scared."

"I will, I promise," Zoe said as she headed down the hallway to Rory's pen with Meep chasing after her.

The little cub was curled up in a heap underneath his blanket with only the tip of his fluffy tail poking out.

"Hi, Rory," Zoe whispered. "Do you remember us? We think we might be able to help. We know you miss your family, and you're feeling really lonely. But there's someone we'd like you to meet — another lion, just like you."

At first there was no movement from the bundle of blankets. Then, very slowly, Rory nudged his head out from underneath. He blinked his brown eyes at Zoe and made a nervous mewing sound.

Zoe shook her head. "I can't take you there yet. My mom won't let you leave the hospital until you eat something. You're very weak, you know."

Meep nodded. "Zoe's right. If you want to meet the other lion, you have to eat first."

The cub raised his paw and patted a piece of meat. Cautiously he started to chew. His ears pricked up and he growled happily.

Zoe grinned as he started to gobble up the rest of the meat. "Mom," she called. "Come and see! I think Rory's found his appetite."

"Rory?" asked Zoe's mom, frowning as she walked down the hallway. "Who's Rory?"

Zoe blushed. "I mean . . . the lion cub. I just thought Rory would be a good name for him. Look, Mom. He's eating!"

"I can't believe it!" she exclaimed. "Well done, Zoe. Whatever you did, it worked!" She crouched down and watched the lion cub enjoying the meat. She smiled. "So you've named him Rory? I like it! You're so good at naming the animals, Zoe."

Zoe couldn't help giggling. Most of the time, the animals told Zoe their names!

"Now that Rory's feeling better, can he

leave the hospital?" she asked, as the cub licked his bowl clean.

Zoe's mom nodded. "Yes, as long as he's still eating well tomorrow. We'll have to keep an eye on the little fellow for the rest of the day," she replied.

"Mom," Zoe said, "I've been thinking. Rory is so little. He needs company, doesn't he? He should live with another lion."

Zoe's mom stared at her for a moment. "You mean Leonard?" she said. "Oh, Zoe, I don't know if that's a very good idea. Lions are usually very sociable animals, but Leonard is so much older and bigger than Rory, and male lions have been known to attack cubs."

Zoe's heart sank. Deep down, she knew her mom was right. Leonard had never

lived with another animal since coming
to the Rescue Zoo — let alone a creature
as vulnerable as Rory. She was so sure
Rory and Leonard would be happy
together, but maybe it was too dangerous
to even try.

She nodded and pushed her hands in
her pockets. Her fingers closed around
something soft and silky — Kiki's feather.
As Zoe stroked it, an idea popped into her
mind. Maybe there *was* a way to put the
two lions together, without putting Rory
in any danger.

Zoe took a deep breath. "I have
an idea," she said. "There's an empty
enclosure right next to Leonard. We could
put Rory in there, just for a little while,
and see if they get along. Even if Leonard
gets mad, Rory will be safe on the other

side of the fence." She gazed pleadingly at her mom. "Can we try it, Mom? Please?"

Zoe's mom paused. "That *does* sound like a good plan, Zoe, but I'm just not sure." She glanced at Zoe's worried face and couldn't help smiling. "Oh, I suppose we've got nothing to lose. OK — let's try it. But not until tomorrow morning," she added as Zoe cheered happily and Meep danced in excited circles on the floor. She picked up her vet's bag. "I've got to go out and check on one of the rhinos now, but I'll see you back home at lunchtime," she said, kissing Zoe on the top of her head.

"And for the rest of the day, I want you to leave Rory in peace so that he can get lots of rest."

"We will, I promise!" Zoe flung herself at her mom and hugged her tightly. "Thank you, thank you, thank you!"

All that afternoon Zoe and the zookeepers worked hard to prepare the empty enclosure for the cub. They built a wooden platform for him to climb on and put up some ropes and sacking for him to play with.

The two enclosures were separated by a tall fence so that Leonard and Rory would be able to see each other, but Rory would still be safe. Halfway along the fence was a wooden door, a little bit like a large cat flap.

Great-Uncle Horace appeared next to Zoe with Kiki on his shoulder. "You've done a great job, Zoe," he said, his kind eyes twinkling. "But I'm afraid that I won't be around to see Rory settling in. I'm going to the Sahara desert to help a very rare black camel. The poor fellow hates getting sand in his face — it makes him sneeze! I hope I can help."

Zoe threw her arms around her great-uncle and gave him a big hug. She didn't want him to go, but she knew that if there was an animal in need, he had to help.

"I know Rory's in safe hands with you." Great-Uncle Horace grinned. "Will you come and see me off?"

Zoe nodded and held on to Great-Uncle Horace's hand as they walked to where the hot-air balloon was waiting.

 97

Meep ran in front of them and Kiki flew overhead.

Zoe watched sadly as her great-uncle climbed into the balloon and started getting ready to take off.

Meep jumped into her arms and rubbed his soft head against her cheek. "Don't worry, Zoe!" he whispered. "Goo will come back soon."

As the balloon lifted slowly into the sky, Great-Uncle Horace waved to the crowd and blew a special kiss to Zoe.

By the time the sun had set over the Rescue Zoo that evening and the last of the visitors had left, Zoe and Meep were exhausted.

Zoe's mom laughed when she spotted Zoe trying to hide a yawn. "Come on, you two!" she said, ruffling Zoe's hair. "Let's get you both to bed. You've been great today."

Zoe brushed her teeth and put on her favorite pajamas, the ones with a pink flamingo pattern. Before climbing into bed, she opened her bedroom window and gazed out over the Rescue Zoo, listening to the gentle hoots of the snowy owls and the howls of the arctic wolves, far away on the other side of the zoo.

"Good-night, Rory," she called softly as she closed the window. "Good-night, Leonard. Maybe this time tomorrow you'll be together. Sweet dreams!"

Chapter Eleven
Rory's Big Day

The following morning Zoe was already up, dressed, and making toast for breakfast by the time her mom came downstairs.

"I can't believe it!" her mom said as she walked into the kitchen. She kissed Zoe and stroked Meep's head. The little lemur was perched on the table, nibbling his second banana. "You're both up so early!"

"I woke up and started thinking about Rory, and then I couldn't get back to sleep," Zoe explained. "And Meep's excited about Rory's big day too." She smiled at her friend as her mom poured herself a glass of apple juice.

Meep had struggled to open his sleepy eyes that morning, but as soon as Zoe had whispered, "*Rory,*" in his ear, he'd become wide awake! Now both Zoe and Meep were desperate to set off and see the little cub.

"Can we pick up Rory from the hospital right away, Mom?" Zoe pleaded.

Her mom nodded. "Of course, sweetheart. We should move Rory to his new home nice and early, before the zoo opens for the day and the visitors start arriving." She finished her juice and spread peanut butter on a piece of toast. "Let's go — I'll eat my breakfast on the way!"

Zoe half-skipped, half-ran to the zoo hospital with Meep on her shoulder and her mom close behind. Rory was already waiting for them. As they raced over to his pen, the cub's ears pricked up happily and he gave an excited growl.

"You've eaten all your dinner from last night," Zoe's mom exclaimed. "Well done, Rory."

"Does that mean we can definitely move him to the new enclosure?" Zoe asked nervously.

Her mom nodded. "Yes, we can. He looks so much stronger already." She smiled at Zoe. "Why don't you carry him there? After all, this is your idea — and Rory seems to like you!"

Zoe grinned in delight. Although she had lots of experience with all sorts of animals, she had never held a real lion cub before. Usually it was her mom and the zookeepers who handled the most fragile creatures at the Rescue Zoo, so Zoe knew this meant everyone really trusted her.

Zoe's mom showed her how to gather Rory carefully into her arms, with the special blanket she'd used when the cub had first arrived. He felt light, soft, and warm, just like a very big kitten. Zoe stroked his silky golden head and he gazed at her with his huge brown eyes. Zoe had never seen anything so adorable — except for Meep, maybe!

With Meep bounding ahead of her, Zoe walked slowly along the path so that she wouldn't drop Rory. This was the first time the cub had gotten a good look at the Rescue Zoo since he arrived, and he sat up in Zoe's arms, staring at the other animals and their beautiful enclosures. Around him, the creatures of the Rescue Zoo brayed, whinnied, roared, and squawked, wishing Zoe and Rory luck.

"Wow, they're noisy today," Zoe's mom said. "It's almost as if they know what's happening!"

As they reached Leonard's enclosure and the empty one next to it, Zoe whispered, "We're almost there now, Rory." The little cub mewed eagerly, excited to see his new home. Zoe saw that a small group of zookeepers had gathered outside to watch.

"Morning," they called in hushed voices, afraid to startle Rory — or to unsettle Leonard.

Zoe could see the old lion through the fence, prowling around and watching them all suspiciously. He looked just as grumpy as ever. Zoe suddenly felt very nervous — she hoped she hadn't made a big mistake.

Zoe's mom used her paw-print pass to unlock the empty enclosure. Zoe bent down and carefully placed Rory inside. As her mom closed the door, they watched the cub closely. Zoe could feel butterflies fluttering in her stomach.

Rory padded straight past the ropes that the zookeepers had put out for him to play with, and went right up to the fence separating his enclosure from Leonard's. His ears pricked up as he saw the lion. Placing a paw on the fence, he growled excitedly.

Zoe glanced anxiously at Leonard. He was watching Rory through the fence. Would he be friendly toward the cub, like Zoe hoped? Or would he growl and bellow and roar? Everyone was silent as the two lions looked at each other. Zoe held her breath . . . until she heard a furious voice behind her.

"*What* is going on here?"

Mr. Pinch glared at them all. His face had turned very pink, which meant he was especially upset. Zoe glanced anxiously at Meep. Was the zoo manager going to ruin everything?

Zoe's mom darted to the front of the group. "I can explain, Mr. Pinch," she said. "Instead of putting the new cub in an enclosure by himself —"

"I can see perfectly well what you are doing," Mr. Pinch snapped. "I do have eyes, you know. What I do not understand is why *I* was not informed first. No animal is to be moved without my permission."

Zoe's mom put her hands on her hips and

took a deep breath. "I am the zoo vet," she reminded Mr. Pinch, "and *I* decided that the cub was ready to leave the hospital. Zoe thought of a really smart way to find out if the two lions could get along by using this empty enclosure."

Zoe's heart sank. She knew that Mr. Pinch would disapprove of the plan even more when he heard it was her idea — and she was right.

Mr. Pinch scowled. "I should have known you two had something do with this!" he sneered, glaring at her down his long, thin nose. "This is unacceptable. It is not up to a little girl and a lemur to decide how my zoo is run!" He turned back to Zoe's mom and pointed a skinny finger at the enclosure. "Remove the cub immediately, please."

As Zoe's mom and the zookeepers
tried to calm Mr. Pinch down, he started
shouting even louder. Inside the enclosure,
Rory growled unhappily. Zoe could tell
all the noise was scaring him. She glanced
at Leonard.

The lion had moved right up to the
fence next to the little cub and was
watching him carefully. Zoe didn't think

he *looked* angry. She couldn't wait any longer. She picked Meep up.

"Meep, listen," she whispered. "Do you see that wooden door halfway along the fence? Can you pull the lever and open it? We need to prove to Mr. Pinch that the two lions can live together. He'll never let us try again, so this is our only chance!"

Chapter Twelve
A Roaring Success

Quick as a flash, the lemur sprang out of
Zoe's arms, darted over to the fence and
pulled the lever. The wooden door swung
open, leading straight into Leonard's
enclosure. Before any of the grown-ups
noticed, Meep ran back to the path and
leaped onto Zoe's shoulder, curling his
tail around her neck.

Rory growled in excitement as he looked into Leonard's enclosure. Zoe's mom glanced up at the noise.

"Oh my goodness!" she cried, her face pale with worry. "Quiet, everyone. Look — the door's open!"

"But . . . how did . . ." Mr. Pinch blustered, his face even redder than before.

Meep chattered innocently.

Zoe crossed her fingers as Leonard noticed the open door and walked through into Rory's enclosure, his yellow eyes gleaming. With a little roar of delight, Rory scampered up to the bigger lion. Zoe's mom and the zookeepers gasped, and even Mr. Pinch was holding his breath.

Come on, Leonard, Zoe thought desperately. *Please don't hurt the cub.*

Rory pushed his golden head against

Leonard's enormous front paw, growling playfully. Leonard opened his huge mouth wide, showing rows of sharp teeth. Zoe gasped in terror as the lion loomed over the little cub . . . and rolled over on to his back with his paws in the air, letting the cub jump all over him!

For a second Zoe just stared at them. Then, as she realized Rory was safe, she threw her arms into the air and jumped up and down in excitement. She felt so happy she wanted to do a cartwheel — or a somersault! On her shoulder, Meep was squeaking and jumping with joy.

"It worked!" Zoe cried, hugging her little friend. "Meep, it worked!"

Behind her, the other zookeepers cheered with relief. Will, the penguin-keeper, shook his head, astonished.

"I just can't believe it!" he said. "I never thought Leonard could be so playful."

"Well done, Zoe," her mom said proudly, wrapping her daughter up in a big hug. "For a moment there I was a little bit worried — but your plan worked perfectly. Thanks to you, both Rory and Leonard have a family now — each other!"

Zoe watched Mr. Pinch stomp away.

"No one ever listens to me!" he snapped.

Zoe's mom smiled. "Don't worry about him," she whispered. "He's just grumpy because he knows you were right! Only someone who *truly* understands animals could have known just what to do." She gave Zoe a kiss. "You'll make a fantastic vet one day."

Zoe beamed at her mom and winked at Meep. She really *did* understand animals — much better than her mom could ever imagine!

From his sunny enclosure, Leonard turned his shaggy head toward Zoe and growled a thank you. Rory copied

Leonard with a baby roar, and patted his new friend with his front paws.

The lion got up and began to show Rory around his new home. They walked through the long golden grass to the pond at the edge of the enclosure which sparkled in the morning light, and after a gentle nudge from Leonard, Rory began lapping at the cool water with his pink tongue.

Zoe grinned happily. "Look, Mom!" she cried. "Leonard's giving Rory a tour!"

"Good old Leonard," her mom said. "Now, the zoo will be opening soon, so I think we should leave our new lion family in peace for a little while. That way they can have a bit of time to settle into their new home together before the visitors start arriving for the day. What do you think, Zoe?"

Zoe nodded. She could happily stay and watch her lion friends all day, but she knew the other animals in the zoo would be desperate to find out if the plan had worked. "Can I go and check on Bella?" she asked. "And Sasha and Oscar and Hetty — and maybe say hello to the otters and the chimps too?"

"Just make sure you're back at the cottage for lunch!" Zoe's mom said, laughing.

Zoe gave her mom a quick kiss on the cheek and waved to Leonard and Rory before dashing off down the path, her dark hair bouncing. Meep leaped along beside her, squeaking excitedly.

"They're all going to be so relieved," Zoe said happily, running her hand over a row of pretty wildflowers lining the path. "And just imagine how pleased Great-Uncle Horace will be when he finds out that Rory has a new family."

"Yes!" Meep agreed. "I hope he doesn't stay away very long this time."

"Oh, Meep, I miss him too," Zoe told him. "I wish we could see him every day! But wherever he is, he's helping scared and sick animals. And the next time he brings an animal home with him, we'll try our best to help — just like with Rory!"

Zoe's eyes shone as she thought about the rainbow hot-air balloon appearing on the horizon once again. "I wonder what the next new arrival will be? Great-Uncle Horace is in the Sahara desert right now, but he might visit lots of other places before he comes home again."

Meep's dark eyes opened wide in excitement. "Maybe another tiny little cat, like Rory!" he suggested. "A baby jaguar or a lynx."

"Or maybe Great-Uncle Horace will bring home something much smaller — like a bamboo lemur? Mom says they're endangered and so, so cute." She winked at Meep.

"Another lemur, like me?" Meep was

so excited at the idea that he bounced around in dizzy circles and almost crashed into a tree.

Laughing, Zoe scooped her little friend up for a hug. As they strolled through the Rescue Zoo, listening to the screeches, barks, squawks, and roars of their animal friends, Zoe sighed happily.

I am the luckiest girl in the world, she thought to herself. *Whatever my next animal adventure is, I can't wait for it to begin!*

New at the Zoo!

Pip is the cutest penguin chick Zoe
has ever seen. But there's something
strange about Pip — he doesn't seem
to know he's a penguin!

New at the Zoo!

Zoe finds out the Rescue Zoo might have to close. She must figure out how to save her home — or the newest arrival, a friendly seal pup, might end up homeless!